Franklin in the Stars

Kids Can Press

FRANKLIN and Harriet loved spending time with their parents. They also loved spending time with their Aunt T.

One night, Franklin and Harriet were very excited. Their parents were going out for dinner — and Aunt T was coming over to babysit.
Franklin and Harriet could hardly wait!

"Hey, everybody," said Aunt T, as she walked in the door.

"Aunt T! Aunt T!" squealed Harriet. "Yay, Aunt T."

Aunt T picked up Harriet and swung her in the air.

"Whee!" shrieked Harriet.

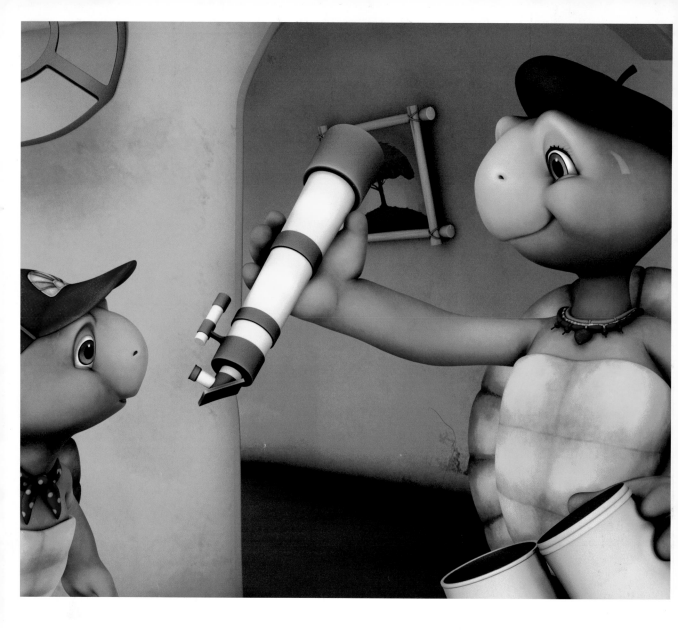

"Hi, Aunt T," said Franklin. He noticed she had a white case in her hand. "What did you bring?"

"Oh, this is my spiffy new telescope," she answered, pulling it out.

"A real telescope? That's so cool-io!" said Franklin.

"A *sillyscope*?" asked Harriet. "Let me see. Let me see!"
"It's a *telescope,* Harriet," said Franklin. "It's for looking at the sky."
"It makes the stars and planets seem really close," said Aunt T. "It's like looking out a spaceship window."

"Can we go outside and try out the telescope?" asked Franklin excitedly.
"You might not be able to see anything in the sky tonight," said
Franklin's father. "I think it's too cloudy."

"Aw," said Franklin with a sigh.

"Cheer up, Franklin," said his mother. "I'm sure Aunt T has something else you can do."

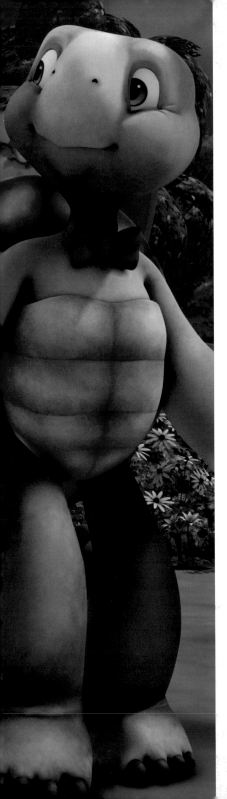

Franklin's parents left for dinner. Franklin looked down at the telescope and frowned. He wanted to look at the night sky more than anything.

"Okay, let the show begin!" exclaimed Aunt T.

"But, Aunt T, we can't even see the stars," said Franklin.

"No stars," said Harriet.

"The whole wide world is a show," said Aunt T. "You just need to find a new way to see it!"

Aunt T took Franklin and Harriet out into the yard. She gave them each a jar. Then she pointed to some lights in the distance.

"Those are fireflies," whispered Aunt T. "I call them 'dancing stars.' Catch them and you'll see why."

Franklin, Harriet and Aunt T caught lots of fireflies. They put them in the jars.

"See?" said Aunt T. "They look just like dancing stars. Let's take them inside."

Once they got inside, Aunt T turned off the lights. Then Franklin, Harriet and Aunt T let the fireflies out of the jars. They flew all around the room.

"Pretty stars!" said Harriet.

"Neat-o," said Franklin. "It does feel like outer space in here!"

"What else would you see in outer space?" asked Aunt T.
"Spaceships!" said Franklin.
"Vroom, vroom!" shouted Harriet.

"You think you could make a spaceship?" asked Aunt T.

"Sure we could!" exclaimed Franklin.

Franklin made his spaceship out of his toy trunk. Harriet made hers out of a laundry basket.

Franklin and Harriet were ready to blast off into outer space. There were just a few things missing.

Franklin gathered a bunch of balls. He painted his soccer ball brown for the planet Mercury. He painted another ball blue for Venus.

Harriet painted a beach ball yellow for the Sun.

Aunt T painted another ball with stripes. Then Franklin put rings on it for Saturn.

And for the Moon, Franklin found a glow-in-the-dark ball!

When Mr. and Mrs. Turtle came home from dinner that night, they couldn't believe their eyes.

It was as if they had entered outer space!

"Wow!" said Franklin's mother.
"I know," said Aunt T with a laugh. "It's out of this world."
"Way, way out," said Franklin's father.

"Come look at Saturn," said Franklin. "It's got rings and everything!"

"I've certainly never seen Saturn up close like this before," replied his father.

"That's because you've never been to outer space," said Franklin.

Just then, a firefly flew past.

"Oh, look!" said Franklin's mother. "There's a shooting star. Make a wish, Franklin."

Franklin closed his eyes.

"I wish for cloudy nights every time Aunt T comes over!"